Happy Holidays!

HAPPY EARTH DAY!

By Alex Appleby

Gareth Stevens Publishing

Please visit our website, www.garethstevens.com. For a free color catalog of all our high-quality books, call toll free 1-800-542-2595 or fax 1-877-542-2596.

Library of Congress Cataloging-in-Publication Data

Appleby, Alex.
Happy Earth Day! / by Alex Appleby.
p. cm. — (Happy holidays!)
Includes index.
ISBN 978-1-4339-9937-6 (pbk.)
ISBN 978-1-4339-9938-3 (6-pack)
ISBN 978-1-4339-9935-2 (library binding)
1. Earth Day — Juvenile literature. 2. Environmentalism — Juvenile literature. 3. Environmental protection — Juvenile literature. I. Appleby, Alex. II. Title.
GE195.5 A66 2014
394.262—d23

First Edition

Published in 2014 by
Gareth Stevens Publishing
111 East 14th Street, Suite 349
New York, NY 10003

Editor: Ryan Nagelhout
Designer: Sarah Liddell

Photo credits: Cover, p. 1 dreamsfolklore/Shutterstock.com; p. 5 Hero Images/Lifesize/Getty Images; p. 7 Lori Adamski Peek/The Image Bank/Getty Images; p. 9 amenic181/Shutterstock.com; p. 11 Robert W. Kelley/Time & Life Pictures/Getty Images; pp. 13, 15 iStock/Thinkstock.com; pp. 17, 24 (recycle) Jupiterimages/Brand X Pictures/Getty Images; p. 19 © iStockphoto.com/Maica; pp. 21, 24 (litter) © iStockphoto.com/vgajic; p. 23 © iStockphoto.com/kali9; p. 24 (Earth) © iStockphoto.com/AntonBalazh.

Printed in the United States of America

CPSIA compliance information: Batch #CW14GS: For further information contact Gareth Stevens, New York, New York at 1-800-542-2595.

Contents

A Day for Earth 4
First Day 8
Cleaning Up 20
Words to Know 24
Index. 24

Earth Day is a great holiday!

It happens every year on April 22.

It started in 1970.

A man named Gaylord Nelson started it.

Gaylord Nelson

People want
to help Earth!

6

They want
to keep it safe.

People like to recycle.

Some people plant trees.

Others clean up litter.

You can help Earth, too!

Words to Know

Earth

litter

recycle

Index

litter 20

Nelson, Gaylord 10

recycle 16

trees 18